Stuck in the Doldrums
A Lesson in Sharing

A CAPTAIN NO BEARD STORY

Carole P. Roman

For David
The best Captain EVER!

Captain No Beard put his finger in the air. He shook his head. There was no wind to move the sails today. He and the crew were on his desert island.

"We are marooned," he groaned. "That means there is no wind, and we will not be moving anywhere today. We are stuck in the doldrums."

"No worries, Captain." Hallie piped in. "We can play in the sand on this beautiful beach."

Mongo peered out of his telescope from the top of a palm tree.

"Just look at those clouds. They look like marshmallows!" the monkey called out.

"Let me see," demanded Captain No Beard.

"No, give it to me," Linus called out, trying to grab the telescope.

"I want it!" Polly shouted.

"Give me the spyglass, Mongo," the captain ordered.

"Not yet," Mongo replied.

"Mongo, I am in charge, so you have to give it to me now," said the captain.

The monkey sighed and slid down the tree.

"Here!" said Mongo, as he stomped off.

Captain No Beard looked and looked but couldn't find any marshmallow-shaped clouds. He did see a sand castle that Linus and Fribbet had built.

"Wow!" he admired it. "That's great."

"Thanks, Captain, here's the drawbridge," Fribbet said.

"Look at my tower," added Linus, who was still working with his shovel to make it perfect.

Captain No Beard walked around the castle. "I think the tower should go here, and the drawbridge belongs over there," he pointed out. He started to rearrange the sand.

"Stop!" Linus roared. "What are you doing?"

Hallie skipped over. "What's happening?"

"We built a sand castle, and Captain No Beard is messing it up," Fribbet complained.

"Avast, mates! You remember, that means stop. I am the captain, so I get to be the boss of everything!"

Hallie, Linus, and Fribbet considered this. Then Hallie said, "Well you are the captain, but I don't think this is any fun." she pointed to the other side of the beach. "Let's go over there and build another castle."

"Fine," No Beard huffed. "I don't need a crew that goes against the captain. It's a mutiny, I say."

Captain No Beard climbed onto the deck of his ship. "Who needs them anyway? It's my ship, and I can do everything myself."

Suddenly, a huge jolt shook the ship, and it rolled back and forth. Captain No Beard felt the deck rocking wildly. "What's going on?" he wondered.

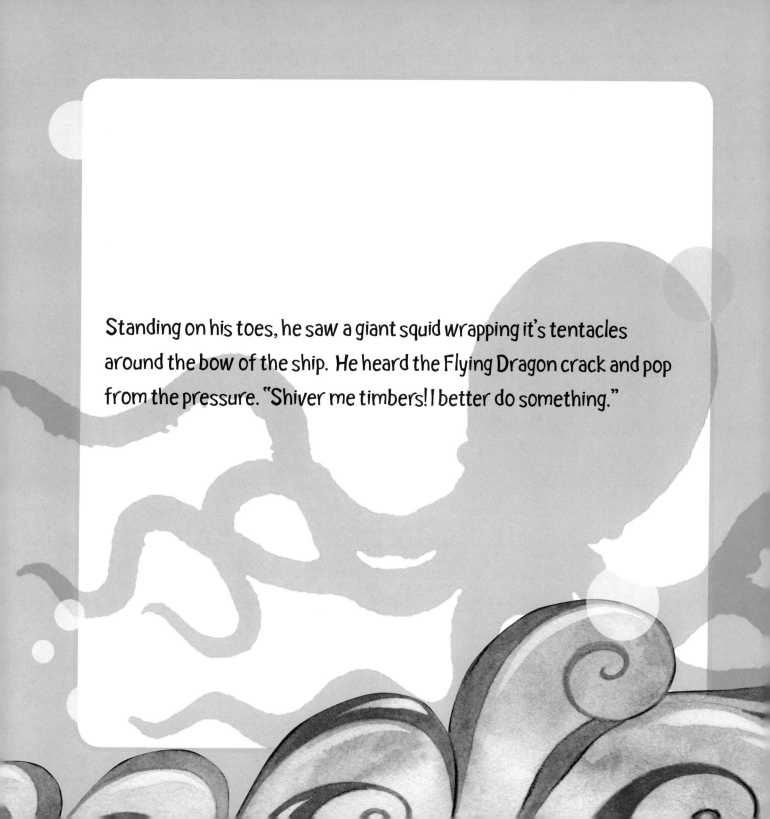

Standing on his toes, he saw a giant squid wrapping it's tentacles around the bow of the ship. He heard the Flying Dragon crack and pop from the pressure. "Shiver me timbers! I better do something."

The captain needed to pull up the anchor and steer the ship away. He couldn't do both at the same time. He could not sail the ship alone. *Captain No Beard needed his crew!*

"Help!" he called out. "Crew of the Flying Dragon, I need help!"

Hallie looked up at his cry. "Captain No Beard needs us. Let's go!"

"No, he was mean," Fribbet replied.

"He took away my telescope," Mongo was still mad.

Hallie looked at them all and quietly said, "We are a crew, and sometimes we don't always get along. First we have to help a friend in need, and we can talk to him afterwards."

"Aye, arrrrgh," they all agreed as they rushed off to the ship.

Captain No Beard sighed with relief when he saw his crew coming to join him. He ran to the wheel. "Man your stations, crew! You all know what to do," he shouted.

Fribbet pulled up the anchor. Hallie and Linus opened the sails. Polly squawked from the topmast, "Hard starboard, Captain." she pointed to the open sea.

Captain No Beard leaned all his weight against the wheel. He felt a breeze whipping up. The ship lurched as wind filled the sails and they jumped free of the giant squid.

"What a team!" Captain No Beard cheered. "I couldn't have done it without you." The crew watched the squid get smaller and smaller as they sailed away. He paused and then added, "I'm sorry for being bossy. Maybe I shouldn't be captain anymore."

"No," Hallie said and put her hand on his shoulder. "You're a great captain. Nobody knows the Flying Dragon like you."

The crew nodded in agreement and Hallie continued, "We like having you lead us. But I think you need *us* as much as we need *you.*"

"I see," said Captain No Beard as he stroked his chin. "Just because you're in charge doesn't mean you know everything. A good captain must consider everyone's feelings, or else nobody will want to be in his crew."

"Arrgh, arrgh," the hearty bunch of mates shouted happily.

And in a flash, the ship disappeared and they were once again in Alexander's bedroom.

"Whew!" Alexander exclaimed as he flopped back on his pillows. "I can tell you one thing, Hallie. Being a captain is hard work!"

"You know what?" Hallie replied. "Being a crewmember is hard work too!."

18407679R00019

Made in the USA
Charleston, SC
01 April 2013